Season of Promise

Elizabeth's Jamestown Colony Diary

· Book Three ·

by Patricia Hermes

Scholastic Inc. New York

Jamestown, Virginia Colony
1610

August 12, 1610, morning

There is much to tell! My heart does leap and dance inside my chest. Caleb is here. My dear, dear twin brother has crossed the ocean safely. He is here with me in the Jamestown fort at last. My baby sister, Abigail, is growing and thriving. And we have food. Imagine that! I am no longer hungry every minute of every day.

But we have different worries now. Our new leaders are stern and they are strong. But they are also sometimes cruel. Just this morning, Lord Delaware did a foul, mean thing. He ordered that Master Brown, one of the few remaining men from our early fort, have his ears cut off! For stealing one cup of meal. I think poor Master Brown did forget. We have food now. There is no need to steal.

But there is no need to cut off a man's ears, either! Inside my head, I told Lord Delaware that. Only Mary, my dear friend, kept me from blurting it aloud.

Later

Oh, but as usual, I talk too much. I go too fast. I even write all of a jumble. I did not tell you who Mary is. I did not tell you who Lord Delaware is. I did not even tell you who I am. But I shall tell you now.

Mary is the best friend anyone could ever have. She is as dear to me as my friend Jessie was.

Lord Delaware is our new leader in the Jamestown fort. He is not at all dear to me.

And I am Elizabeth Mary Barker. I am one of the first girls ever to live in the Jamestown fort. I am ten years old. I am not at all proper, though I do try. I talk too fast. I walk too fast. I talk too much. I even blurt out things I should not say. But I am trying to learn to be better. I really, really am. I am doing it because my dear mama would have wanted me to.

More later. Papa is calling me to help him mend the roof.

August 13, 1610

This is my third diary. I tell it everything that I think and do. That way, Caleb and I can look back and remember. Also, when Abigail is big, she will know how it was. And she can know something about her dear mama. So each diary becomes like a best friend. So now, my dear diary friend, I shall share a secret.

Once, John Bridger did try to steal and read my diary. So I discovered a code. I do that when I have something very secret to tell you.

Irunmywordstogetherlikethis.

August 14, 1610, nighttime

It is dark. All of the Jamestown fort is quiet. Caleb lies on his bedroll beside me. Papa is in his bed in the corner. Baby Abigail sleeps in her cradle, breathing her sweet baby breaths. Caleb and I whisper together. He has been separated from me for one entire year. So he has a hundred thousand questions for me. Yes, I kept a diary for him. Still, he wants to hear every single thing. He asks about our journey here. He asks about the Indians and their queer ways. He asks about Pocahontas, my Indian friend. He wants to know the names of the birds. He asks about Captain John

Smith, our first leader here. He asks about Captain John Ratcliffe and Francis West, leaders here who squabbled like children. And who abandoned us. He especially wants to know every single thing about dear Mama.

But now, Papa whispers to us from across the room, "Hush."

Baby Abigail sighs in her sleep.

We hush now. We shall wait till Papa is asleep. Then we shall talk more. I still have almost a hundred thousand questions to answer.

Later

An owl hoots from the tree outside. The moonlight is so bright through the open door that I see my shadow. And Papa snores. Now Caleb and I sit up and talk again. One year ago, Mama and Papa and I crossed the ocean to this Jamestown colony. Caleb was left behind in England, for his lungs were weak. We came looking for a new life here. In England, life was hard. Papa was a third son. He had no land. We had been promised land and riches and gold here. We did not find gold. We did not find riches. We found sickness. And fear. And near starvation. We found that we must live inside a fort.

Wait! Baby Abigail cries out. I must go soothe her before she awakens Papa.

Later

Abigail had lost her thumb. I put it back in her mouth. She sleeps now.

More about our coming here: Our leader, Captain John Smith, knew how to work with the Indians. He was also a strong leader of men. But then, he was injured. He had to return to England last autumn. After he left, the people squabbled. Men refused to work. Even Papa could not get them to work. Our food supply dwindled to nothing. We became so hungry we ate worms. And dogs. And worse! A terrible sickness swept the fort. Indians attacked. So many died. We started out with five hundred people. When Caleb's ship and the others arrived this spring, we were but sixty. Our mama was one of the many who died. Even now, months later, my tears wet the page. Caleb and I hold hands.

Midnight

I open my book again and write in the moonlight. For Mama would want me to record this, too: We also found good things here. There is land — beautiful, beautiful land for the taking. There are trees and blue waters and fish and birds. And flowers. How I love the flowers! There is laughter. And I have new friends. Even some Indian people are friends. I tell Caleb how an Indian brave did save my life and that of many others this winter. Caleb laughs loudly when I tell him that I told that Indian brave to mind his manners.

Oh, dear! Papa is wakeful again. He again says, "Hush." He says it like this: "HUSH!"

We hush.

August 15, 1610, morning, the sun peeps over the trees

Papa and Abigail still sleep. Caleb sits up, rubbing his eyes. He wants to hear again about my ocean crossing and the hurricane. That was the storm that caused some of our ships to be lost. He thinks it wild and thrilling. I tell him that story gives me shivers. I also tell him I do not understand boys. Why must they always feel wild and thrilled?

He squints his eyes at me. He folds his arms and pretends to be angry. I fold my arms. I pretend to be angry back. But we are both smiling.

Church bells ring. Time for morning duties. More later. Abigail is squalling like a mad crow.

August 16, 1610

Papa hurries off to work. Papa does not interfere in the politics here. But he has always been a leader. He is also a master carpenter. So now he is in charge of the men who are rebuilding the chapel. Before winter comes upon us, Lord Delaware has ordered that the chapel, the storehouse, and the houses all be rebuilt. He has also ordered new streets laid out. And we must strengthen the walls of the fort. The well, too, will be cleaned. All these things fell into disrepair this past winter. There was no food, so men were too weak. And the sickness killed so many. But now, with the supplies Lord Delaware has brought, no one goes hungry. There are also more supplies on the ships from Bermuda and we are all well fed. All this makes Papa happy. He says idleness is what caused our fort to almost fail. Everyone has work now. Even me. More later.

August 17, 1610

I am most happy to have good, hard work. I wish to show Caleb all that I have learned here. Girls work every bit as hard as the men. Well, some girls do. I even helped build our house!

August 18, 1610

This is my first task each morning: I take Baby Abigail to Mistress Whistler to be nursed. Mistress Whistler has no children. Her poor baby died at birth, just before Abigail was born. And our mama had no milk, as she herself was dying. So Mistress Whistler nursed Abigail, and did save her life. Yet I cannot help hoping that soon, Abigail will no longer need to nurse. I do not much care for Mistress Whistler. She is a silent, grim woman. Though I know I should be grateful to her.

Caleb's morning task is to collect firewood. He must leave the fort to do that. Some say that is dangerous, for there are Indians about. But after that Indian saved my life, I do not think I shall ever fear an Indian man again. Still, I do feel happier when I see Caleb safe inside the walls again.

August 19, 1610

I must tell you how the fort looks now. It is shaped like a triangle, with three long wooden walls. In two of the walls, there are gates. One gate faces out to the river. One faces the forest. This past winter, much of the wall fell down and became rotted out. But now, many men are building it up again. They do that because some think the Indians are our enemies. The fence will keep them out. But the fence also keeps us in! Sometimes I feel caged up.

Papa says the Indians are a lot like the rest of us. Some are good. And some are not so good.

August 20, 1610

I realize that I have forgotten to tell you about Pocahontas. She is the daughter of the

Indian people's chief. She is a bit older than me. She is brave and wild and beautiful. She befriended us in our time of need. It is she who helped Captain Smith in his dealings with the Indians. But all this past hungry winter, she did not come to visit. We still do not know why.

August 21, 1610

I write while I wait for Baby Abigail to nurse. Mistress Whistler looks like a buzzard with her shoulders hunched up over Abigail. She rarely speaks, and when she looks at me, she squints up her eyes as though she is studying me. I think that she thinks that writing is frivolous. My mama did not think so. But Mistress Whistler is not at all like Mama. She is very, very bossy. Today, she had many commands for me: *Elizabeth, fetch water and wash your hands. Elizabeth, your cap is soiled. Elizabeth, what is that flower doing poking out of your pocket? Elizabeth, it is not proper for a girl to bury her face in a book. Elizabeth, Elizabeth, Elizabeth!* One day I shall simply change my name. Then I can pretend that I know not to whom she is speaking.

August 22, 1610

Now listen to this! Mary called me to her this day. She took me to our old hiding place. It is behind the well. The weeds grow tall there, and we see no one around. It has been our meeting place for almost a year. She had a secret to tell. But oh, it is so delicious, that I shall make you wait. I shall tell the secret tomorrow.

August 23, 1610

Was it cruel to tease you so? But this is just too good: There is a new girl here. Her name is Temperance Flowerdew. Is that not a beautiful name? And Temperance *is* beautiful, as lovely as a flower. She came on the ship from Bermuda. She and Mary have shared some happy moments together. And we, the three of us, have chosen to become best friends. We shall tell one another everything. Both Mary and Temperance are older than me. But we shall be like sisters now.

I am so happy to have another best friend.

August 24, 1610, morning, while I wait for Abigail

Oh, I am so angry I shall burst. No, I am so angry I shall spit. Maybe even I shall spit *and* burst! Mistress Whistler says that our leaders have made a new rule. It is this: Girls may no longer work alongside the men. Instead, we must sew and cook and gather herbs. Yes, and we shall do the washing! And we may draw water from the well.

Abigail is still nursing. Mistress Whistler is still squinting at me. I shall run to Papa and ask what he knows. This cannot be true.

Later

I met Mary on the way. And it is true! Mistress Bartlett told her so. And Mistress Bartlett would not lie. Oh, I feel rebellious. I do despise the task of stitchery. I hate to cook. The only pleasant thing about washing clothes is getting wet in the river. When Captain Smith was in charge, he and I worked side by side building houses! I built and thatched roofs. I repaired buildings and the walls of the fort.

Oh, why do our new leaders treat us like children? We have survived things that most men cannot.

Still later

I ran all the way home to tell Papa. He was not at home. But Caleb is. I know I must be all red in my face, I am so angry. Caleb is angry for me. He tries to soothe me. He calls me by the pet name that Papa calls me — Sweet Beth. We shall climb and thatch the roofs again, he says. Together, he says, we shall sneak out into the forest. We shall climb things and play and shout and swing on vines. For we are not afraid of Indians.

His words make me smile. I do believe he is the sweetest boy in the whole wide world. He makes me think of Mama.

Nighttime

I have had a terrible thought: I think I may know how this rule came to be. You see, one recent day, Lord Delaware was striding about the grounds of the fort. He was with his guards. He was dressed in his long red cloak though it was one hundred degrees! And I — I was not dressed in a fancy red cloak. I had tied my skirt like trousers, and I was working. I was atop our roof with Papa, mending the thatch. Caleb was handing up nails and supplies. Lord Delaware almost swooned when he looked up at me there. He stared. He did not speak to me. But he spoke to the guard by his side. I do believe now that it is because of me that he made that rule.

Ihopehetripsonhiscloakandfallsonhisnose.

August 25, 1610

Today I am feeling very cross still. Stitchery. We girls must stitch today. We shall mend breeches and repair sails for ships and all the things this fort does need. Since I have no mama, nor does Mary, Papa sends us to the home of Mistress Bartlett. Each day she gives us tasks to do. Abigail stays with Mistress Whistler. And Caleb goes with Papa and Mary's papa to rebuild the church. I do admire Mistress Bartlett, for she is a kind woman. When her children are sad, she says, "There, there, little ones, don't fret." And I have never heard her scold. She is also very kind to me. I think she knows it is hard to have no mama. Sometimes, she does touch my face, most gentle like. Just as she does to her own children. But she makes me stitch and sew! And I would do most anything than stitch and sew.

Iwouldeveneatwormsagain.

August 26, 1610

I must tell you about the Bartlett family. They came on the ship with Caleb under the command of Lord Delaware. There are almost thirty of them. With Master and Mistress Bartlett are their seven children, six boys and one girl. Mistress Bartlett's two sisters came with their husbands and children. Master Bartlett's mama and papa came also. They have built four houses, side by side. They all are most devout in their ways. And mostly, they are very jolly. Even the boys are kind. Caleb and the son Joshua have become close friends. But the girl, Sarah, the youngest, I do dislike intensely. I suspect she does not think much of me, either.

August 27, 1610

More about Sarah. She does not speak to Mary nor to me. When we pass her by, she pulls her lovely English skirts closer to her. It is as though she thinks we are blacksnakes. And then she makes a small, quiet sound like this: *Tsk, tsk.* Mary and I have named her Miss Tiskit.

She is small and fragile, like a little bird. A pretty little bird. Her hands and feet are tiny. And her skin is white and fair.

Mary and I are both so brown and thin, we must look like savages. Though we are both fattening up prettily. At least, Mary is getting pretty. I am afraid I am quite plain.

Nighttime

Still thinking about Miss Tiskit. I know it is wrong to think vain thoughts.

ButIdowishIwerepretty.

August 28, 1610

I feel strange inside sometimes. I feel different from the new children here. I even feel different from Caleb at times. I think it is because only those of us who lived here truly know how it was this past winter. We care about different things now, important things.

But still, I am envious of Miss Tiskit.

August 29, 1610

Oh, today I am happy. Because Temperance also comes to Mistress Bartlett's to sew and quilt. While we stitch, we talk. I have not yet told you about Bermuda. Well, how could I? I have not been there. But Temperance tells us all about it. It seems to be an island of beauty and grace and warm climes. And there is always plenty to eat. The people are beautiful — that is, if they all look like Temperance. It sounds like Paradise. I cannot believe such a land exists. She says most solemnly that it does. The weather is always fair. There are blue seas and white sands. And fruit and coconuts and vegetables grow in abundance. There are fish for the taking, and even wild boars for meat. Best of all, it is always summer there. And there are flowers everywhere — even more than here.

Oh, but I did not tell you how she came from there to here.

More next time. Mistress Bartlett reminds us to stitch, stitch, stitch!

Later

It was the hurricane that brought several of our ships to Bermuda. The hurricane hit all nine of our ships of the Third Supply in the middle of the ocean. The waves took us up and up and up. We seemed to be like birds, flying right up to heaven. And then the waves slammed us down. Waves towered above us like the cliffs of England. My friend Jessie and I clung to each other. Papa used strong ropes to tie us to the ship as waves washed over us. We were scared most to death. We tumbled back and forth across the deck like small wet rats.

Miss Tiskit laughed at this.

I stopped and stared at her.

After our noon meal

Temperance begged me to go on. I took a deep breath to calm myself. Then I told Miss Tiskit that she would not have laughed had she been there. For many sailors were washed off the deck and into the sea, never to be seen again. When light dawned and the seas quieted, men wept openly. For some of our ships were lost. The supply ship, the *Sea Venture*, was lost. It held our food and many of our leaders. It was not seen again till this summer. And do you know where the ship came to land? In Bermuda. Was that not a fortunate thing for those men to live in such a land? They spent many months building new ships, the *Deliverance* and the *Patience*. Then they sailed here last spring. And that is the story of how Temperance Flowerdew came to us.

I think she was most fortunate. I think I am fortunate to have her here.

More later. I must now get Abigail from Mistress Whistler.

Evening

Mistress Whistler sat in her open doorway. She was sewing something out of lovely pale blue wool. Abigail was at her feet, banging an iron pot with a large wooden spoon. For a moment I watched them. They looked so much like a little family.

It made me lonesome for Mama.

Later

I have brought Abigail back home. She rides on my hip, one arm around my neck. I picked a flower for her, and she holds it tightly. She is so sweet, as she pats her little hand on my back. I have taught her to say "Papa." She says it like this: *Papapapapa!* I teach her to say "Elizabeth." She tries. But it sounds like this: *Lilbit*. She cannot say "Caleb" at all. Instead, she calls him *Coocoo*. I do not think *Coocoo* sounds at all like Caleb. But perhaps it does when one is only ten months old.

August 30, 1610

Early morning. The sun is not yet up. But Mr. Bartlett is at our door in the dark. He calls Papa to him. They speak quietly a moment.

They both seem most distressed. Papa hurries away with him. But first, Papa tells me to stay and care for Abigail.

I know that children are not welcome in the affairs of grown men. But as soon as they are out of earshot, I shall follow on tiptoe. It is not really disobedient, for I shall take Abigail with me.

I shall tell you what I find.

Later

Nothing! That is what I found. What I saw was Papa and Master Bartlett reading something posted on the walls of the fort. But I could not get close enough to see. And when Papa turned back, I had to scramble for home. I bent low under the trees. I hurried home like a little mole. Abigail squealed at being bounced around so as we ran. But I reached home before Papa. And when I asked, he told me nothing. All he would say was, "Later, Elizabeth."

Why does he treat me like a child?

Later still

Papa and Caleb have gone off to their work on the chapel. I must take Abigail to Mistress Whistler. Then I shall go to my own work. First though, I shall return to the wall. Most girls my age cannot read. And many grown women cannot read. But Mama taught me in London before we came here. And I am a good learner.

Mistress Whistler once said that I was nosy. I think I am just inquisitive.

I shall read what is posted on that wall. Then I shall tell you what I learn.

Even later

Still nothing! I was not able to get close enough! There were many men gathered at the wall and there was much muttering. One man, a gentleman, Sir Thomas Gates, laid a hand gently, but firmly, on my shoulder. He asked if I did not have a task to do. I said I did, and I hurried off. But now, I am plotting inside. I shall find a way to see what is written there. Perhaps Mistress Bartlett knows? I shall ask, though perhaps she will not tell.

Why do the adults keep secrets from children? We always find out, anyway.

At Mistress Bartlett's

Mary and I offered to draw water from the well. Mistress Bartlett was pleased to allow that. So we went, but of course, we had a plan.

It was to read the posted messages. We were so bedazzled by the news that we returned to the house — without the water! So now we shall return and draw up water. More later.

Much later

Now I know and I shall tell you here. This is what is posted on the walls of the fort. They are the new rules made up by our rulers.

If a man steals bread or food, he will have his ears cut off.

If he should do it a second time, he shall become a slave for a year.

If a person does anything against the known articles of the Christian faith, he shall have his head cut off.

If one misses three Sunday services without permission, one is to be put to death.

Mary and I did stare wide-eyed at each other. My heart was pounding fiercely.

I do believe our Lord Governor is mad. Or perhaps he has turned feebleminded. I was about to say so to Mary. But there is another rule. And this one kept me silent:

Death to those who speak disrespectfully of the Lord Governor.

I may not speak with disrespect. But I shall write anything I wish. And what I wish to write now is this:

Ihopeyoufallinthewell.

And if you climb out:

Ihopeabeareatsyouup.

Mid-morning

When we returned, Mistress Bartlett saw that we were distressed. She said not to fear.

Those rules are only for those who cause tyranny in the fort. They are not intended for children. But I think this: Papa is not a child. Mistress Bartlett is not a child. Master Bartlett is not a child. And Mary — Mary is fifteen. Is she a child still? And Temperance Flowerdew is surely not a child.

Of course, none of them would steal. But what if they make a small mistake? Or what if they are caught speaking disrespectfully? It is enough to make one wish for the return of Captain John Ratcliffe and Francis West. They were weak leaders. They squabbled. They left the fort when we needed them. But they did not put men to death.

I do believe that I shall speak out. And then what?

August 31, 1610

I have been thinking and thinking. I know that this past winter, there were no rules. Men were lazy. Some said they were gentlemen and they refused to work. Men stole food and fought one another. They kept Indian people as slaves. And so — we starved. And died.

Those were terrible times.

Now, we have rules and men work. There is food. People are healthy and well. But the rules are so harsh and one can get put to death for the smallest things. Surely there is a better way to rule than these two ways.

I remember John Smith telling me, "Why, Elizabeth, I do believe you should help me govern." Perhaps I should. Because even I could do better than Lord Delaware is doing!

Later

I saw Master Brown today. Remember I told you — he was to have his ears cut off for stealing food? But he is still walking around with his ears on. I wonder what that means. Could it be that the rules will not be enforced? I hope they will not.

Evening

Oh, yes they will. Caleb told me. He heard it at the church at his work. He says that soon the whole fort will be summoned together. We shall be made to watch Master Brown have his ears cut off. That is to make an example of the poor man. Oh, I will never watch such a thing. If I am forced to go, I shall squeeze my eyes shut. And if they say that I must open my eyes, they will have to cut off my head to make me do it.

September 1, 1610, a new month

I did tell you about the kindness of Mistress Bartlett. But how can such a kind woman have such a horrid little child? Little Miss Tiskit heard me speak of my fears to Mary. And listen to what that horrid Miss Tiskit did say. Just guess! She said, "Why, Elizabeth, I do believe you are quite cowardly."

Later

Oh, I am still raging inside. I would like to see Miss Tiskit survive our past winter. I would like to see Miss Tiskit eat bugs and worms as we did. I would like to see her meet up with Indians in the forest. I would like to see her deal with the death of her own ma . . . .

No, of course I do not wish that. I shall not

think that. I shall try to be kind and forgiving. As my own mama would have wanted.

Butlfeelanythingbutforgiving.

September 2, 1610

Oh, I am so humiliated. I met Lord Delaware in the town square this day. Actually, I did not meet him. I crashed into him. *Smack*, just like that. I was not looking. I was running. I had picked some wildflowers and was taking them home to put in a jug. I smacked him so hard that he fell over backward!

I cried out an apology. And then, I did bend down and give him my hand. He took it and let me help him up. His lovely cloak was all muddy. I thought that perhaps I should try to dust him off. But, of course, I thought better of that. Oh, it was so humiliating. I stood there, my eyes cast down. Then I had a horrid thought: Perhaps I would be put to death?

I looked up at him.

And do you know what? He looked most surprised. But he was not angry! He just shook his head. And with a wave of his hand, he sent me on my way.

Evening

I told Mary and Temperance to meet me in our secret place. We met at sundown. I told them what had happened.

Mary gasped and her eyes got wide. Temperance looked frightened, also.

Mary stared at me. Was it really true, had I really run into him? She made me repeat it, as though she could not believe it.

I said sadly that it was true.

Temperance shook her head at me. She, too, made me repeat it. Had I *really* knocked him over?

I assured them that I had. I said that I did smack him so hard, he fell down on his bottom.

And then, suddenly, Mary began to smile. Temperance began to giggle. And I must admit, I, too, began to smile. Suddenly, all three of us were laughing. We laughed and laughed and laughed. But after a minute, we stopped. We became most serious. We looked at one another. And then we laughed some more!

It has been many weeks since there has been such laughter in this fort.

Caleb laughed, too, when I told him. Right away, he got his sketchbook and drew a quick few lines. He turned his book so I could see. When I saw what he had sketched, I laughed all over again. It showed our Lord Governor in a most undignified pose.

Late evening

I wondered if perhaps I should hide what happened from Papa. I thought perhaps he would be angry. Yet I knew he would hear it from someone. So tonight at supper, after our meal of fish stew — about the only thing I can cook that one can eat — I told him. And, oh, my dear, dear papa! He laughed as hard as Mary and Caleb and Temperance. He leaned close. He told me, "Sweet Beth, many people wish they could do what you have done."

Oh, I do so love my papa!

September 3, 1610

Most days, while Abigail nurses, I take a moment to write here. This day, I pushed aside the blue wool on the table, to make room for my diary. A bit of ink from my quill fell on the wool. Mistress Whistler was very angry. "Now, look what you have done!" she said. I said that I was sorry. And I was. It is such lovely wool. Mistress Whistler then sent me out of doors. She bade me empty the pail of nighttime slop. I had to carry it outside the walls, for that is a new rule. Our "necessities of nature" must be done outside the fort. I dared not leave my journal behind so I did tuck it inside my apron. I did what I was told. But inside myself I told her: You are *not* my mama.

September 4, 1610

Today, Mistress Whistler bade me bring a message to my papa. She wishes to speak with him this evening. I hope it is not about the ink spot I made on her wool. I also hope it is not about a different matter of worry to me. You see, I sometimes note a certain look in Mistress

Whistler's eyes. It is much like the look Mary did have when she loved that dreadful John Bridger. I have an awful fear. I fear that Mistress Whistler does wish to marry my papa.

Later

When I returned home, Papa was not yet here. I told Caleb about the message. And about my worry. Caleb does not know Mistress Whistler as I do. But he says if I do not like her, he could not like her, either. Yet we both know that Papa feels grateful to Mistress Whistler.

We think perhaps I shall forget to give Papa this message.

September 5, 1610

Mistress Whistler was stitching that pretty blue wool when I arrived this morning. She put it aside and reached for Abigail. She seemed more quiet than usual. I kept my eyes down and did not tarry. I simply left Abigail and went on to Mistress Bartlett's and my work. I wonder if Mistress Whistler wonders why Papa did not come to her.

Later

Oh, I fear! I fear. When I arrived at Mistress Bartlett's this day, she had a summons for me — from Lord Delaware. I am to go to him when the noon bells ring. I must have paled, for Mistress Bartlett said I should not fear. She says she will go with me if I am truly afraid.

I turned and saw Miss Tiskit smirking at me.

So, of course, I said that I was not afraid. I will go alone.

But, oh, I am afraid. Am I to be put to death?

Late morning

Before I left, Mary held me to her. It was a long, silent hug. Now, I sit for a moment on a log and write here. I tell myself that I have done scarier things than this before. The only problem is — I can't think what those things might be.

Noon

The noon bells are ringing. I shall stand up and tuck my diary in my apron. I shall dust dirt from my skirt. I shall straighten my cap. And I shall pray. I recall that I have forgotten to pray in recent days. I am praying hard now.

Late day at home

When I came into Lord Delaware's presence, I found him seated at a long table. Two of his Halberdiers were by his side. He sent them away. He bade me sit down.

I did. But I did not dare raise my eyes. I waited for him to speak. While I did, thoughts raced around like tiny moles inside my head:

I am young, younger than he. I can run fast. I can escape over the walls of the fort. I can live in the forest. Or perhaps with the Indians. I can find Pocahontas, my Indian friend. I can outrun his guards if they do chase me. But what if I never see Papa and Caleb and Abigail again and what if . . .

I looked up. And do you know? Lord Delaware was smiling at me. He did *not* say that he would put me to death. But he did say many things. I shall tell you later. (I am not teasing you here. It is that Abigail is howling for her supper.)

Evening

Abigail sleeps in her cradle. I sit by the open door, for it is still awesome hot here. And now I shall tell you what Lord Delaware said to me. He said that he had heard many things about me. At first, I thought he meant bad things — such as climbing roofs, and perhaps saying evil things about him. But no. He said he had heard good things about me. He heard that I am strong. I am brave. I helped save this fort during the starving time. He says I am the kind of child this New World needs. The other children here, he says, are all silent and dull.

Well! Of course we are silent! *We are scared to death of having our ears or heads lopped off!* But for once, I was struck dumb.

I was so awed I simply said nothing. He said that perhaps in a fortnight or two I would return to talk to him. He almost commanded me to have something to say next time. I think he thinks now that I am as silent and dull as the rest of them.

Well, of course, I have something to say. But I do believe that my dear mama would have been happy with me. For once, I did not blurt out words without stopping to think. I do wish to hold on to my head. With my ears still attached!

September 6, 1610, morning

Oh, Caleb is so excited for all the good things Lord Delaware said about me. And Papa just stared in surprise. But — he did not tell me what to say when I return in a fortnight or two. He says that I shall find my own words. But I know not what those words will be.

September 7, 1610

Mary and Temperance met with me at the well. We three have many ideas of things to tell Lord Delaware. We have made up a list.

1. He should shed his silly red cloak. We think *he* thinks he is the king of the New World.
2. He should disband his guard of Halberdiers. They resemble foolish peacocks, anyway, the way they strut about the grounds in their cloaks. Also, I would like a bit of that red velvet for a dress — though I surely would not say that to Lord Delaware.
3. He should make the church services much shorter.
4. He should start schools for boys — *and* girls!

5. He should have picnics and songs and playtimes for the children.

Oh, we have many silly thoughts.

But can I say the important thing? Can I really say that he should not put men to death? Do I dare speak up? I am but a child.

Later

But I am a strong child. He said that his own self.

Later still

A strong, scared child.

September 8, 1610

I will not think too hard about it. I will let thoughts play around in my head. I have weeks and weeks. Perhaps he will even forget about me. And if he does not, then something will come to me.

I hope.

September 9, 1610, morning

It is so hot here. Won't autumn ever come? As we stitched this day, Temperance told us more about Bermuda. She promises that this is true — women do not wear many clothes and petticoats and shifts. They wear thin skirts and thin gowns. And their feet are often bare.

Miss Tiskit shook her head and made her *tsk*ing sounds. She said that she would never be so bold. I believe she says that because she has lovely English clothes. She makes sure I notice each new dress or apron. She has at least six gowns! This day, she wears a thick woolen skirt. She wears an apron. And I see a shift, maybe two, peeping out beneath her skirt.

I cannot help but smile, though. Her face is red and shiny with heat and sweat.

September 10, 1610

Another day of sun beating down. And no rain at night to cool us off.

Mistress Whistler is still silent. She does not order me about. But she still squints up her eyes at me. She takes Abigail and holds her close. She has not asked about the message. But I see her looking at me as though she wishes to speak. I think perhaps she is too proud to ask.

My heart is hurting inside me. I fear I have done wrong.

Later

Gowns. Why do I care about gowns and such? I have food. That is what is important. But somehow, when we stitch together at Mistress Bartlett's, I see what others wear. Today, Temperance wore a dress as lovely as any I have ever seen, even in England. It was rosy red with ribbons and tiny, tiny buttons all down the front. I feel ashamed because my dress is plain and my apron, too. Yet at least I have a dress — two dresses! Mistress Bartlett stitched them up for me as soon as she arrived here. I am afraid that I was dressed in tatters.

At times like this, I miss my own mama terribly.

September 11, 1610

Thoughts about Lord Delaware run around and around in my head. I think: If an opportunity presents itself, perhaps I could make things better here.

Then I think: or perhaps I could lose my head!

September 12, 1610

Oh, I think my heart will break! This day, Abigail wrapped her little arms around Mistress Whistler's neck. Then Abigail said a new word. She said, "Mama."

Later

So many things happening.

Temperance whispers to Mary and me that

she has a secret to share. We shall meet by the well at dusk.

I have to decide whether I dare speak plainly to Lord Delaware.

Abigail still calls Mistress Whistler Mama. Mistress Whistler does not meet my eyes when Abigail says that. Could it be that Mistress Whistler knows how I feel?

And my heart does hurt about that message. Perhaps I shall tell Papa. And say that I did forget?

I feel all mixed up inside.

September 13, 1610, morning

This is the secret that Temperance shared with us: She says that she does hope to marry. There is one here whom she loves. But, mean thing, she will not tell us who it is! Mary and I think we know, however. For we see her blush in the presence of George Yeardley. He is a pleasant man. But I do not think him handsome. Should I ever marry, my husband shall be handsome.

Just think — were he not, I might have ugly children. For I know that I am plain. I told Mary. She just smiles. She says, just you wait. Someday you will be grown and beautiful. I blush, for I know it is wrong to be so vain.

ButIstillwishthatIwerepretty.

AndIwishIhadoneprettydress.

September 14, 1610

I gave Papa the message from Mistress Whistler. I said the message was days old. I am afraid that I did lie. I told him I had forgotten. Papa did not seem angry. He says he will go to her tonight.

Oh, I do hope Papa does not choose Mistress Whistler!

Evening

Papa has gone off to speak with Mistress Whistler. Caleb and I huddle on the doorstep. I rock Abigail in my arms. She pulls the edge of her blanket to her face and sucks on her finger. I can see that she will soon sleep. Caleb makes pictures in his sketchbook. All three of us are very quiet. Even the birds no longer call to one another. It is as if the whole fort is settling down to sleep. Or to wait.

Later

Abigail sleeps. Caleb and I talk softly. Caleb says Papa will not marry Mistress Whistler if we do not wish it. I say he shall. I know it is hard to be a widower in this land. One needs a wife for so many things.

Caleb says that perhaps one might also need a husband. We both sigh.

It worries me. And I do not understand myself. Mistress Whistler has been most kind to us. So why do I dislike her? Is it just because she squints up her eyes at me? Or is it because I think she does dislike me, too?

A quick note before bed

When Papa came home, he was humming softly. He admired Caleb's drawings. He put a hand on my head and called me Sweet Beth, his pet name for me.

Oh, dear. I do think that means he is happy.

September 15, 1610, morning

Though it is September, it is still blazing hot. Still, we see hints that autumn will come. In the forest, leaves are turning red and gold. They whisper in the breeze. Squirrels scurry about, busy hiding nuts. Caleb makes many sketches of the animals here. He sketches the Indian people, too. Some of the Indians are beginning to visit us again. They did so when Captain John Smith was here. But after he left, they did not come for a long time. Now each day, one or two return.

September 16, 1610

Today, many Indian men and women and children came to the fort. They brought gifts, wild turkeys and game, and a fat fish in a basket. We think perhaps they came to say farewell. Soon they will leave for their winter grounds. I looked for the brave who did find me in the forest on that mad, sad day. And saved my life. But I was so ill and feverish that I have little memory of his face. Besides, they all seem tall and fierce, though I know now their hearts are good. Some of the men wore feathers in their hair. The women wore colorful beads. And the small children wore hardly anything! The Indian braves wear little, too. At first, that made me blush. Now, I feel that they are far smarter than we.

Nighttime

Oh, how could I forget this? Pocahontas came, too! Caleb thinks she is very beautiful. She spoke sweetly to him, for she speaks

English as well as we do. But she has changed. She did not climb trees nor turn somersaults. She seemed to be like a grown woman.

It made me feel shy.

September 17, 1610

Today, the sun is so hot I think my shoes will melt. When Mary and I went picking wildflowers, we both took off our shoes. But I made sure to mark where I had left them. Once before, I lost my shoes. Mama became most angry then. And though she is no longer with us, I try to do as she would want. I also know now how important certain things are here — things like shoes. One cannot just go to a shop as we did in England and buy new ones! Though I wish we could. Then I might buy a new gown.

September 18, 1610

Today, again, we sew. I do try to make even stitches in my work. But my stitchery is so bad, Mary is forever helping me. I cannot even run one single straight line. Today, I pricked my fingers so often, the cloth ran red with my blood. Mary sighs and says, "Oh, Elizabeth, if you would just go slow." I tell her she speaks just like my poor dead mama.

For a moment, that made us both sad. But not for long, for Mary has a buoyant nature and laughs much.

As for me, my poor fingers do look like pincushions.

September 19, 1610

I know it is George Yeardley that Temperance does admire. I note that he comes often into the room where we stitch. Temperance then looks down at her stitchery. She does not glance up. But she gets a lovely, sweet blush on her cheeks.

Today when he came, I did look at him. He smiled at me. I stepped on Temperance's toes. She squealed and gasped. Master Yeardley asked if she were ill. She shook her head hard. But she still did not look up. And her cheeks turned the color of a ripe eggplant.

Afterward, she was angry with me. She says I brought notice to her. Indeed, I just kicked her so she would look up. I told her I did not understand. If she does love him, then why not look at him?

She says that someday I will understand.

I do not think I ever will.

September 20, 1610

Last winter, Mary did love John Bridger. Poor John is dead, though I must admit I do not miss him much. He was a horrid boy who stole my journal and stole our food.

I told Mary that I do not understand girls and boys. Caleb is the only boy I could ever love. And he is my own brother. She says that when I am older, I will love someone else. She also says that I will understand how Temperance feels now. I am tired of being told that I will understand later. It seems they all treat me like a child.

September 21, 1610

We all put in small gardens this summer, and they are prospering. Soon it will be time to begin drying the herbs for winter. And, of course, there are still wild herbs to gather. This morning, Mistress Bartlett asked if I would gather herbs for her. I was so pleased and said that I would happily do so. I did not say that I would rather do anything than stitch. Though, of course, she knows. She had to wash my blood from the shirt I mended yesterday.

But then Mistress Bartlett said that Sarah — Miss Tiskit — would accompany me!

Grrr! I feel as grumpy as a bear. But then, I think, perhaps it will do Sarah good to get her pretty hands soiled. It might be most interesting to see how she behaves. I shall let you know.

Noon

Can you believe this? When it was time to pick herbs, Miss Tiskit pretended to be feeling poorly. But her mama just said, "There, there, you will feel better out in the sunshine." So off we went.

But guess who picked and gathered the herbs? The lavender and picklewort and rosemary and thyme? Well, of course, you know who. Me!

And guess who sat on a log pretending to be ill with stomach cramps?

Yes. You are right. Miss Tiskit. I didn't really expect anything different. But at least I did not have to sew.

Later still

When I finished with the herbs, I thrust the herb basket into Miss Tiskit's hands. And I went off to pick a bunch of wildflowers. And then — guess what again? Miss Tiskit ran off home. She presented the herbs to her mama as though she had picked them all herself!

When I came back later with the wildflowers, Mistress Bartlett was quiet. I felt she was disappointed in me.

How could I say what a sneak her daughter was? I could not. So I did not say anything. But I shall get even!

Evening

I do believe I will not need to get even! I believe that Mistress Bartlett knew who gathered the herbs. Perhaps she saw Miss Tiskit's white, clean hands! At any rate, early this evening, Mary and I saw Miss Tiskit in her garden, cutting rhubarb. Her fingers were filthy. There were streaks of green soil and mud across one cheek. Her cap had fallen back on her head, and her hair was wet with sweat.

Mary and I looked at each other. We quick

put our hands over our mouths. We turned away, laughing.

If Jessie were here, she would tell us to be kind. But at times like this, I like Mary better.

Sheisalittlebitmeanlikeme.

September 22, 1610

Men are working at cleaning the well. Lord Delaware and his men think the well water may have caused our sickness. They think it got spoiled from deep underground. Because we all did our necessities of nature inside the walls of the fort. Now we must do our necessities outside the walls of the fort. In the daytime, that is fine. But what about when nature calls after dark? I do not want to meet owls or blacksnakes or even Indians in the dark. I make Caleb come with me if I really must go. Meanwhile, we keep a pail in a corner of the house. Sometimes, it becomes most unpleasant.

September 23, 1610

Temperance and Mary and I worry that our hiding place will be revealed. But so far, our secret place is still safe. It is far behind the well in the weeds. None of the men seem to have noticed the worn path we have made. No one comes here but us — and lately, blacksnakes. We carry sticks now. We have become adept at lopping off snakes' heads. Do you think the snakes fear us as we fear Lord Delaware? But these snakes are poison, Papa tells me. And men are not like snakes.

ExceptforLordDelaware.

September 24, 1610

Mistress Whistler does not order me about so much lately. Yet I note that she watches me closely. Sometimes, the looks she sends me are sad. I wonder what has passed between her and Papa. And why she seems so sad and quiet. She has also put away her pale blue wool. She sits with her hands in her lap quietly. Yet Papa seems more cheerful. I do not understand.

And Abigail still calls her Mama.

September 25, 1610

I have not gone to Lord Delaware. He has not sent for me. Shall I go? Shall I stay? What shall I say?

I think for now, I shall just do nothing.

September 26, 1610, the Sabbath

I am properly dressed and ready for church services. Soon, Papa and Caleb and Abigail and I shall walk together. We do not meet in the church yet, for the repairs are not complete. Instead, we have services in the log house that has been built for Lord Delaware.

Every Sabbath, the service is so long and so dreary. Is it wrong to think so? I have to pinch myself to stay awake.

Later

Today was like every other Sabbath. There are hours and hours of talk and prayer. And more talk and more prayer. Reverend Buck says the same words over and over again. Week after week. He says, "We must revere God's mercy for sustaining this colony." *Well, yes, I* think. But surely God heard you the first time! Baby Abigail squirms and wriggles on my lap. I become so hungry that my stomach rumbles and makes embarrassing noises. Papa frowns at me, though I see a smile in his eyes. And I think: *Surely God does not want us to starve to death in church.*

Home at last

We are home! Service was long, long, long as usual. Abigail fell asleep. Sometimes I wish I were a baby. No one tries to awaken her. But should I fall asleep, there are men whose job it is to keep us awake. They poke us with long sticks.

I do not believe the Lord means for us to be poked with sharp sticks. Do you?

September 30, 1610

Outside, birds are waking. One bird sounds forlorn and seems to call its mama. It cries like this: *Mimi, mimi, mimi*. It says it over and over again. I wonder if its mama hears.

Evening

Tonight at supper, Papa was in high spirits. He said that his work crew had completed the windows of the chapel. Caleb and I begged to go see and Papa agreed. Caleb took his sketchbook. I put Abigail in her sling on my hip. Papa took my hand, and we walked together under a dusky blue sky, tinged with the reds and pinks of sunset. And oh, the church is beautiful! The windows are large and wide to let in light. The chancel is made of cedar. It is so fragrant. And the communion table, Papa says, will be of black walnut. It is not yet finished. But it will be most beautiful. It *is* most beautiful. It is enough to make one's spirits soar right up to God. I stood and looked through the wide windows, at the stars just beginning to peep out of the night sky. And I did whisper a prayer of thanksgiving.

October 1, 1610, a new month

Oh, dear. Guess what? Just when I have become certain that Lord Delaware has forgotten his summons, he spoke to me as we left the church last evening. He said he would summon me soon. Perhaps this coming week.

Oh, help!

Later

Mary says not to worry. She says I should just speak my mind.

Ha! And be put to death?

Later still

Caleb says so, too. *Speak your mind!* He points out that Master Brown still has his ears. So perhaps it is mostly talk?

I do not know.

October 2, 1610

Is it just the success of the church building? Or is it something else? Papa seems happy. It is the first time since Mama died that I have seen him really happy. Even after Caleb came, Papa still seemed held by sadness. Now he hums and smiles to himself.

So why does that worry me?

You know why.

October 3, 1610

This morning, I brought Abigail to Mistress Whistler again. Abigail crowed and tumbled from my arms into the outstretched arms of Mistress Whistler. Then, she buried her little face in Mistress Whistler's bosom.

I watched. And felt my heart do something strange. Again.

October 4, 1610

I had pricked myself for the hundredth time this morning. Miss Tiskit was beside me. She was sewing very tiny stitches. She looked at the shirt I was mending. She rolled her big eyes, and looked at me so sweetly. But there was meanness in her sweet eyes. I bit my lip and did not say a word. Mistress Bartlett saw, though. Perhaps she saw the tears in my eyes, though I tried hard to keep them back.

She patted my hand softly. She said so quietly, "There, there." For a moment, I felt that I had a mama again.

Afternoon

At last, I am free! Free of needles and stitchery. It happened this way. After Mistress Bartlett patted my hand, she said that there will be no more stitchery for me. I shall do other things. I can work in the garden. I shall gather herbs all day. She will teach me how to cook. I turned up my nose at that. But I know that I will need to know if I am ever to be a wife. Also, Caleb and Papa will be happy to have something besides stewed vegetables and fish stew — the only things I can cook now.

So now, I am as happy and free as a bird.

I still await a summons from Lord Delaware, but I shall not let it take away this happy feeling. For now.

Evening

Caleb says that Mistress Whistler must be a good woman to do what she has done.

She is a good woman, I am sure. But good enough to be a mama? To be *our* mama?

October 5, 1610

Oh, how lovely the world seems this morning. I came to Mistress Bartlett, and right away, she sent me out into the garden. She says I may pick and weed and sing if I wish. And best of all — Mary will work with me!

I must admit I was puzzled. And I blurted out, "But why?"

Mistress Bartlett did not answer. She just smiled.

Mary and I do not know. We know only this: She is a wonderfully kind woman.

P.S. Even though she has a horrid daughter.

Noon

Just before noon, we stopped to rest a moment. Miss Tiskit came from the house with a jug of cool water for us. She did not smile in her usual mean way. In fact, she did not smile at all. Her look was calm. Even polite. She simply offered us the water and two cups. And then she returned to the house.

Now what am I supposed to think?

October 6, 1610

Tonight, when Papa came back from his work on the church, he gathered Caleb and me to him. He said he had something important to tell us. My heart thudded into my throat.

Yes. He said what I thought he might say. He is thinking of asking to marry Mistress Whistler. He asked what we did think.

Caleb looked at me.

I looked at Caleb.

I closed my eyes. My mama's face flashed across the insides of my eyelids. I saw her when she breathed her last, her eyes fixed on the ceiling.

Would she want Abigail to grow up without a mama? I wondered.

I quick opened my eyes. Where had that thought come from?

Papa was looking at me. Caleb was looking at me. I swallowed hard.

"If you wish, Papa," I said.

Papa and Caleb both smiled.

October 7, 1610

This morning, everything was all of a jumble. I awoke late. I could not find my clean shift. Abigail soiled herself just when I was ready to take her to Mistress Whistler. I had to stop to change her. I could not find the ink for my journal. I was later than usual arriving at the home of Mistress Whistler. She was standing at the door, looking for us. Seeing her there, I wondered: *Can I ever think of you as Mama? Shall I call you Mama?* I can never do that.

Mistress Whistler held out her arms for Abigail. Abigail was grinning with her one tiny tooth sticking up. She reached out and tumbled into the arms of Mistress Whistler.

Each time that happens, my heart does ache inside my chest. And I miss my mama so.

Later

Papa says he has spoken to Mistress Whistler. She has agreed to be his wife.

October 8, 1610

Papa and the men have repaired the church tower. They have hung two huge bells there.

The bells ring every noon and in the morning and evening. They summon us to prayer and to work.

It is a sweet and holy sound.

I wonder if they will ring for Papa's wedding vows.

Later

I told Mary. She remembers my dear mama. She puts a hand on my arm. She says perhaps it will be all right.

Temperance says there is this to think about: Perhaps I shall get a new baby brother or sister now.

I blush to think that. But it might be sweet for Abigail to have a baby to play with.

I shall try to feel content.

October 9, 1610

I am so ashamed. I am so, so ashamed I can hardly write here. Tears fall on this page. More later.

Later

I still find tears falling from my eyes. But I am not sad. Just . . . something! I do not even know what I feel. So I guess I must just put it all on paper. Because putting it on paper seems to clear this foggy, silly head of mine. I shall do it in the morning, when my brain is fresh from sleep.

October 10, 1610, early, early

The sun is just peeping over the horizon. Everyone still sleeps. So I shall tell you now why I feel the way I feel. All muddled up in my head.

Yesterday, Mistress Whistler handed me a basket. It was covered with a small cloth. She said to take it home. Then to look inside.

I thought perhaps it was food for us and Papa. But it was not food at all. It was a gown! For me! It is made from the soft blue wool that she has been stitching. She has not been staring at me meanly, as I did think. She has most likely been studying me for size! The gown fits perfectly. And it is so beautiful, with tiny tucks down the front and a ribbon on the bodice! I could not even find the ink stain I had made. Though I did look. Oh, now do you see why I feel so ashamed of my mean, mean thoughts?

Later

There is more. There was a note in the basket. It said this:

Dear Elizabeth,

I am sorry if I am not jolly like your own mama. I remember her well. I loved her, too. I will not try to be your mama. You already have a mama, in heaven.

You know I do love Abigail. I hope that I can come to know and love you. And your brother.

I hope that you will learn to like me a little bit.

Love,
Anna Whistler

P.S. You need not call me Mama. Perhaps just Anna will do?

Later

Church repairs are not yet complete. But the roof no longer leaks. The windows are in.

So today will be the first service in the church. I hope the seats are more comfortable than the ones in the log house. Sometimes I think my bottom has turned to stone. I thought to wear my new blue gown. But I decided to save it for the day of Papa's wedding vows.

Late day

Listen to this! This is how Lord Delaware arrived at Sabbath service today. He strode into chapel. He looked neither right nor left. He marched up the aisle. He was accompanied by a guard — fifty Halberdiers in red cloaks. I counted. *Fifty!* He settled himself in the choir. The men lined up on either side of him. He sat in a green velvet chair that had come on board ship with him. There was a velvet cushion placed before him — to protect his poor knees when he knelt!

Heads turned and people whispered.

I sent a look to Mary.

She sent a look back.

We each knew what the other was thinking: He does indeed think he is king of the New World!

October 11, 1610

Tomorrow I must go to Mistress Whistler in the morning. What shall I say to her? How shall I thank her? Shall I ask her forgiveness?

October 12, 1610, early morning

Abigail made it easy. When I brought her to Mistress Whistler, she tumbled from my arms. But she would not go to Mistress Whistler. Instead, she wanted to be on the floor. She balanced herself on her little fat feet. She wobbled a bit back and forth. And then she did take her first step!

Oh, we were so happy! Mistress Whistler and I both clapped and cheered for her. And do you know what? Abigail began to cry! I think we frightened her.

I scooped her up and hugged her till she stopped sobbing. After she had quieted, Mistress Whistler touched my shoulder. She said softly, "You are a good mama to her."

Yes.

I took a deep breath. And then I said, "You are, too."

October 17, 1610

Oh, I can hardly believe what I have done. I daresay you will not believe. But it is true. I was summoned to the home of the Lord Governor. He talked and talked. He talked for a very long time. I think he just likes the sound of his own voice. But I did tell him something, too. And I still have my head. More later. It is time to fetch Abigail.

Later

Soon, I shall not have to bring her to and fro. Mistress Whistler — Anna? — will live right here. I still hardly know how I feel about that.

Evening

More about Lord Delaware. You know how sometimes you meet people and do not like them? But then you talk awhile, and find they are quite pleasant? That has happened to me often. Can you believe that Jessie and I did not like Mary at first? Well. I just tell you that to explain something. I hoped that might happen with Lord Delaware. But it did not. I still do not admire him. I still think he is pompous. And cruel. But for some odd reason, he talks to me.

Wait! I must scoop up Abigail.

Just now, she almost walked into the fire. I have placed a chair to block her off. Perhaps it will be good to have Mistress Whistler — Anna — live here. I won't have to spend my whole day chasing Abigail. She just learned to walk! And now she seems to want to walk all over the place. I have given her a spoon and a stick to keep her happy.

Almost suppertime

Now, about Lord Delaware. He seems to dislike the children here. He thinks about a school — but just for boys! He says we have all become silent and dull. And then, oh, I could not help myself! I told him it was not lack of schooling that makes us silent and dull. It is that we are afraid.

He waved his hand. He seemed to think that was not a matter of interest.

"Is fear not enough?" I answered. I am afraid that I said it in a most spirited way.

He stared at me. I was so angry I did return his look. I did not let my eyes fall.

And then do you know, he dropped his eyes. He nodded.

So I dared again. I told him how cruel it was to cut off men's ears — and heads. I told him that poor Master Brown is ill in his head. He is not responsible for stealing.

Lord Delaware stayed silent. Shortly after, he sent me on my way. And I still have my head. (Ears, too.)

October 18, 1610, suppertime

Oh, I am so glad that Mistress Wh . . . I am trying to remember to call her Anna . . . will take over the cooking. Tonight, I made stewed vegetables. Again. It is not so hard to do. But why does my stew look — and taste — like stewed soil? Oh, wait! Abigail has wandered out the door.

October 22, 1610

Papa and Mistress Whistler will be married next week. There will be no big ceremony. Just a small exchange of vows with the Reverend Buck. Mary and Temperance and I are making a wreath for Anna's head. (There! I remembered to say her name.) It will have lavender and birch leaves and sprigs of rosemary, for those will smell sweet and pungent all at once.

I shall wear my precious blue dress.

Caleb does not care much about clothing. But tonight he is brushing his one good pair of breeches.

October 30, 1610

Oh, such a day! Listen! Miss Tiskit came out into the garden again today with fresh water for Mary and me. She did sit herself on a bench and spoke quietly. We all talked of this and that — flowers and herbs and ships and gardens and Indians. She did not say a single mean word. Even her looks were not mean.

I did not know it was possible for people to change. Well, I guess I knew. But I often forget.

I shall try to be nicer to Miss Tiskit even in my thoughts. Perhaps I shall begin to call her by her real name now. Sarah.

October 31, 1610

For the wedding we shall decorate the chapel with wildflowers, armloads of wildflowers and bright fall leaves. Mistress Bartlett says I may take as many of her flowers as I wish. Of course, Miss Tiskit — Sarah — had something to say about that. (She has not changed *completely*.) She says the Lord Governor will be displeased. There have never been flowers in our church, she says.

I told her I am not bringing flowers for Lord Delaware. I am bringing them for God. And for Papa and Anna.

Oh, I have to tell you, it might seem that this could not happen. But I assure you it did. As I walked to Mistress Bartlett's this morning, I was stopped by one of Lord Delaware's Halberdiers. He had a message for me from the

Lord Governor. He bent close to me. He said this: "Master Brown shall not be punished."

That was the entire message! And then this Halberdier disappeared — almost as quickly and as silently as the Indian braves do disappear. I wonder if he felt frightened. For I admit, I did jump about and dance like an Indian child myself.

November 1, 1610

Another new month — and another day of joyous news — for this be the day that Papa did marry.

Anna — and there, I wrote her name again! — looked sweet and flushed. Her eyes actually sparkled. In chapel, Abigail was quiet for once, just looking around. And Caleb and I did stand by Papa's side.

After the vows were said, we helped Anna bring her few things to our house. She has a chair and a stool and a table. And a bed! Now Caleb and I need not sleep on a bedroll. We shall have our own bed. For Papa already has a bed to share.

Then, we walked together to Mistress Bartlett's, where she had prepared a wedding supper.

Late night

Just a quick note. It was so, so wonderful. Mistress Bartlett's house was crowded with people. So many here admire my papa. He has quiet, strong ways. And do you know — Lord Delaware did also attend the supper! He complimented me on the flowers in the chapel. He said that from now on, we shall always have flowers in the chapel.

I was too awed to speak. Imagine. Me silent? More in the morning.

November 2, 1610, early, early morning

I was too tired to write more last night. But now listen to this. Just as Lord Delaware was leaving, I followed him out of doors. All in a rush, I did speak. I felt I just must thank him for pardoning Master Brown. So I did. And then do you know what? He said almost the very words that Captain John Smith did say! "Elizabeth," he said, "I do believe you could help me govern. You would govern wisely!"

Me? Govern wisely? I am a foolish child. I am a child who speaks without thinking, and is mean-spirited besides. At times.

But . . . could it be that I am learning?

Late November, 1610

Winter is coming on. I have not written here in weeks. I have been so busy harvesting our small crops and gathering and drying herbs. Anna is teaching me to cook. She does not even try to teach me to sew. She says there is plenty of time for that. We talk sometimes, about the bad, hard time when she lost her husband and her poor baby. And I lost my dear mama.

It is good to have someone else here who remembers.

Late December, 1610

Christmas has come and gone. Mary and Temperance and I exchanged small gifts. Mary did give me a lovely ribbon for my hair, and Temperance gave me a prayer book. Anna helped me bake small raisin cakes for each of my friends. And guess what? The cakes were actually edible!

Mary is in love again — this time with Jacob Bartlett. She says that they will marry. That means Miss Tiskit — Sarah — will be Mary's new sister. But we think that will be all right. Sarah has learned to mind her tongue. Somewhat. And I am learning to be kind to her. Somewhat. Temperance is to be married in the spring to George Yeardley. I guess she was finally able to look at him!

A new year — again! 1611

There is a rumor that soon Lord Delaware shall leave us. George Percy then shall be the new governor. It seems to hardly matter. We are thriving now. We hear of no more men being put to death. We also hear that new ships will arrive soon. Papa says that the fort may grow to many hundreds, thousands even.

I tell Papa that I cannot picture that many people, not even in my dreams. Papa smiles at that. He says that is because when your life is so small, living in a small colony such as ours, then you begin to dream small.

Now, says Papa, in this new year, we can begin to dream large again.

Late February, 1611, dark and cold

Caleb and I sit and talk by the fire in the evenings. Papa mends shoes or reads, and Anna sews. It is clear now that Papa is content. And Anna is a good enough mama. She is not so sharp and impatient with me. Maybe that is because she, too, is content. I notice her belly is swelling. Caleb and I think that someday there will be a new brother or sister for us. Abigail is growing and learning all sorts of new words. Mostly she has learned to say, "no!" Caleb and I talk about being grown up. Caleb's drawings are so beautiful. We think that one day he will be a famous artist or cartographer.

And me? Well, perhaps I shall write famous books and diaries. Or perhaps I shall govern a colony someday! Papa says that is not an impossible dream for a girl to dream.

Oh, and one further thing. Caleb and I both feel sure of this: Somewhere in heaven, Mama still looks down at us. We think what she sees does make her happy.

Historical Note

In the winter of 1610, after its first leader, Captain John Smith, left Jamestown, the colony faltered and almost disappeared. That time was called the Starving Time, and during that winter, with no real leadership, hundreds of settlers eventually died of disease and starvation, after having been so hungry that they ate dogs and worms and worse — anything to try to keep alive.

Settlers of Jamestown.

When supply ships — built from the remains of the shipwrecked and long-missing *Sea Venture* — finally arrived from Bermuda the following spring, with food and medicines and supplies, only around sixty-five people were on hand to greet them. At first, the remaining settlers begged to leave the town, and they boarded the ships, sailing upriver toward the sea. However, at the mouth of the river they spotted new ships on the horizon: ships from England, bearing

new men and fresh supplies. The settlers rejoiced, and the fleeing ships turned back to Jamestown, where a new leadership was installed under Lord Delaware (whose original title was

Lord Delaware. Thomas West, Lord de La Warre).

Once again the town thrived, church bells rang out, and people were fed. But the rule of Lord Delaware was harsh. Men were put to death for the smallest infractions — three absences from church services without an excuse was considered cause for death — and the town breathed a sigh of relief the following summer when Lord Delaware returned to England. A new leader, George Percy, took over for a time, but then he, too, fled home to England. His rule was followed by that of Sir Thomas Dale.

All of these men had harsh temperaments, but as a result the colony grew and prospered for many years. Eventually Jamestown became the first capital of Virginia. Another "first" occurred in 1619 when the House of Burgesses convened there, the first representative legislative assembly in the New World.

Jamestown in 1619.

About the Author

Patricia Hermes is the author of more than thirty books for children and young adults. She has written four other books for the My America series: *Our Strange New Land* and *The Starving Time*, which are the first two stories of Elizabeth Barker's experiences in the Jamestown Colony starting in 1609, as well as Books One and Two of Joshua's Oregon Trail Diaries, *Westward to Home* and *A Perfect Place*. Many of her books have received awards, from Children's Choice awards to state awards, ALA Best Books, and ALA Notable Book awards.

Acknowledgments

Grateful acknowledgment is made for permission to reprint the following:

Cover portrait by Glenn Harrington.

Page 104: Settlers of Jamestown, North Wind Picture Archives.
Page 105: Lord Delaware, North Wind Picture Archives.
Page 106: Jamestown in 1619, by S. E. King, Photograph by
          T. L. Williams, Williamsburg.

Other books in the My America series

Corey's Underground Railroad Diaries
by Sharon Dennis Wyeth
Book One: Freedom's Wings
Book Two: Flying Free

Elizabeth's Jamestown Colony Diaries
by Patricia Hermes
Book One: Our Strange New Land
Book Two: The Starving Time

Hope's Revolutionary War Diaries
by Kristiana Gregory
Book One: Five Smooth Stones
Book Two: We Are Patriots

Joshua's Oregon Trail Diaries
by Patricia Hermes
Book One: Westward to Home
Book Two: A Perfect Place

Meg's Prairie Diaries
by Kate McMullan
Book One: As Far As I Can See

Virginia's Civil War Diaries
by Mary Pope Osborne
Book One: My Brother's Keeper
Book Two: After the Rain

For Elizabeth Mary Nastu

-̃⟨ ⟩̃-

**While the events described and some of the characters in this
book may be based on actual historical events and real people,
Elizabeth Barker is a fictional character, created by the author,
and her diary is a work of fiction.**

Copyright © 2002 by Patricia Hermes

Library of Congress Cataloging-in-Publication Data

Hermes, Patricia.
Season of promise / by Patricia Hermes.
p. cm. — (My America) (Elizabeth's Jamestown Colony diary ; bk. 3)
Summary: In 1610, ten-year-old Elizabeth continues a journal of her experiences living in
Jamestown, as her brother Caleb rejoins the family, a new, strict governor comes to the
colony, and her father considers remarriage.
ISBN 0-439-38898-8 — ISBN 0-439-27206-8 (pbk.)

1. Jamestown (Va.) — History — Juvenile fiction.
2. Virginia — History — Colonial period, ca. 1600–1775 — Juvenile fiction.
[1. Jamestown (Va.) — History — Fiction.
2. Virginia — History — Colonial period, ca. 1600–1775 — Fiction.   3. Diaries — Fiction.]
I. Title.   II. Series.
PZ7.H4317 Se   2002
[Fic] — dc21   2001058536
CIP   AC

10 9 8 7 6 5 4 3 2   03 04 05 06

The display type was set in Caslon Antique.
The text type was set in Goudy.
Photo research by Dwayne Howard
Book design by Elizabeth B. Parisi

Printed in the U.S.A.   23
First edition, November 2002